Anna, Banana,

and the
Recipe for
Disaster

Anna, Banana,

and the
Recipe for
Disaster

Anica Mrose Rissi

ILLUSTRATED BY Meg Park

SIMON & SCHUSTER
BOOKS FOR YOUNG READERS
New York   London   Toronto   Sydney   New Delhi

SIMON & SCHUSTER BOOKS FOR YOUNG READERS
An imprint of Simon & Schuster Children's Publishing Division
1230 Avenue of the Americas, New York, New York 10020
This book is a work of fiction. Any references to historical events, real people, or real places are used fictitiously. Other names, characters, places, and events are products of the author's imagination, and any resemblance to actual events or places or persons, living or dead, is entirely coincidental.
Text copyright © 2018 by Anica Mrose Rissi
Illustrations copyright © 2018 by Meg Park
All rights reserved, including the right of reproduction in whole or in part in any form.
SIMON & SCHUSTER BOOKS FOR YOUNG READERS
is a trademark of Simon & Schuster, Inc.
For information about special discounts for bulk purchases, please contact Simon & Schuster Special Sales at 1-866-506-1949 or business@simonandschuster.com.
The Simon & Schuster Speakers Bureau can bring authors to your live event. For more information or to book an event, contact the Simon & Schuster Speakers Bureau at 1-866-248-3049 or visit our website at www.simonspeakers.com.
Also available in a Simon & Schuster Books for Young Readers hardcover edition
Book design by Laurent Linn
The text for this book was set in Minister Std.
The illustrations for this book were rendered digitally.
Manufactured in the United States of America
0218 OFF
First Simon & Schuster Books for Young Readers paperback edition March 2018
2 4 6 8 10 9 7 5 3 1
Library of Congress Cataloging-in-Publication Data
Names: Rissi, Anica Mrose, author. | Park, Meg, illustrator.
Title: Anna, Banana, and the recipe for disaster / Anica Mrose Rissi ; Illustrated by Meg Park.
Description: First edition. | New York : Simon & Schuster Books for Young Readers, [2018] | Summary: "Anna must whip up a new cookie recipe for the bake sale when her jealousy of Sadie and Isabel's new friend has her exaggerating her baking skills"—Provided by publisher.
Identifiers: LCCN 2017002857 (print) | ISBN 9781481486743 (eBook) | ISBN 9781481486729 (hardcover) | ISBN 9781481486736 (paperback)
Subjects: | CYAC: Jealousy—Fiction. | Best friends—Fiction. | Friendship—Fiction. | Cookies—Fiction. | Baking—Fiction.
Classification: LCC PZ7.R5265 (ebook) | LCC PZ7.R5265 Anw 2018 (print) | DDC [Fic]—dc23
LC record available at https://lccn.loc.gov/2017002857

For Henry and Emmett
—A. M. R.

Chapter One
Batter Up

"No, not the carrots!" my best friend Sadie said to the television. "Don't add those to the cake batter! Yuck!"

My other best friend, Isabel, shrugged at the screen. "I like carrot cake," she said.

"Yeah, but *chocolate* carrot cake?" Sadie said. "Blech. No thank you." We watched as the kid contestants on *The Batter-Up Bake-Off Show* grated three large carrots into the mixing bowl and poured in a cupful of chocolate chunks. Sadie wrinkled her nose.

"I'd try it," Isabel said. "What about you, Anna?"

"If Dad served it for dinner, I'd have to," I said. That was the food rule at my house: You eat what you're served, even if it's beets or brussels sprouts.

"True, but you're at my house now," Sadie said. "There aren't any rules like that here." There weren't any food rules at either of Sadie's houses. Both of her parents let her eat what she likes. And here at her dad's place, we're allowed to watch as much TV as we want, too, although usually we're busy with games or adventures.

Hanging out at my house is still the most fun though because there we get to be with my dog, Banana. But Banana doesn't mind if I go to Sadie's or Isabel's, as long as I tell her all about it afterward.

"I'd still probably try it," I said, "if only so I could tell Banana what it tastes like."

Sadie shuddered. "Just let her taste it for herself!"

"Nope. Chocolate is really bad for dogs. Like, it's basically poison," I said. I was always super careful to keep chocolate out of Banana's reach. Even the thought of her eating some made my heart skip with panic.

Isabel nodded. "Cats too," she said. "We thought Mewsic maybe ate some once, and had to take him to the vet." Mewsic is Isabel's gigantic orange tabby cat. He's even bigger than Banana.

"What did the vet do about it?" Sadie asked.

"She gave him some medicine to make him throw up," Isabel said.

"Aw, poor kitty," I said, trying not to picture it.

"Yeah, but at least then he was safe," Isabel said. I couldn't argue with that.

"Oooh!" Sadie grabbed the remote and turned up the volume. "This is my favorite part."

It had been Sadie's idea for us to watch TV today—she'd really wanted us to see this new baking show. "Batter up!" she cheered, along with the whole TV audience. On screen, the two teams of kid contestants stepped up to the judges' plate to show off their final creations.

"Whoa, they sprinkled carrots on top of the frosting, too," I said, as that team gave the "pitch" for why their recipe invention should win. "They're really into this chocolate-carrot thing."

Sadie stuck out her tongue. "Gross."

"I like it," Isabel said. "It looks like a Halloween cake."

"Yeah, but Halloween is over." Sadie leaned back into the couch where we were sitting. "I think the other team should win. Zucchini-walnut cookies sound much better, even though it's still vegetables for dessert."

"I'd at least give the carrot team points for creativity," I said.

"Definitely," Isabel agreed. But the judges agreed with Sadie. They awarded the golden chef's cap to the other team.

"We should go on this show together," Sadie said, clicking it off with the remote. "We're a really good team."

"But we don't know how to bake!" Isabel said.

"So? We'll learn." Sadie tossed a throw pillow at me and I caught it. "I'm going to a cupcake-making party tomorrow after school, actually," she said.

Isabel perked up. "You're going to Monica's birthday party? Me too!"

"Cool!" Sadie said. She and Isabel beamed at each other.

I looked back and forth between them, feeling suddenly left out. "Who's Monica?" I asked. I didn't know Sadie and Isabel had a friend in common who wasn't me.

"A girl in Mr. Garrison's class," Sadie said. "I

don't know her all that well, but her mom and my dad work together, so that's why I got invited."

"I was friends with her last year in Ms. Lahiri's class," Isabel explained. "Before I met you guys." Sadie and I had been friends forever, but we only met Isabel this school year. It already felt like we'd been friends with her forever too though.

"Oh. I think I know who that is," I said. I could picture Monica's short, curly hair and big brown eyes, but I wasn't sure if I'd ever talked to her. Even though we were the same age, we had never been in the same class. Of course she hadn't invited me to her birthday party—we didn't even know each other. But it was weird that Sadie and Isabel would be going to the party without me. I couldn't help feeling sad about that, but I tried not to show it. "A baking party sounds fun," I said.

"I'm so glad you'll be there," Sadie said to Isabel. "I thought I wouldn't know anyone."

"I'll sit next to you!" Isabel said. She turned to me. "Once we're baking experts, we'll teach you everything we know."

"Yeah!" Sadie said.

I hugged the throw pillow to my chest and tried to ignore the lump in the back of my throat. It wasn't anyone's fault I was being left out—that was just the way it was. And it was only for one afternoon. Still, as my Nana would say, it was a bitter pill to swallow.

I forced myself to smile. "As long as you won't be hiding any carrots in the cupcakes," I said, and tossed the throw pillow back at Sadie.

Sadie laughed. "No way."

Isabel held up her hand for a three-way pinky swear, and Sadie and I hooked our pinkies with hers. "Only sweets in our treats," she said. "We promise."

Chapter Two

A Spoonful of Envy

The next morning when I got to school, I spotted Isabel out on the playground, sitting on her favorite reading rock. She was so wrapped up in the story she was reading, she didn't seem to notice me, even once I was standing right in front of her.

"Ahem," I said to get her attention.

Isabel's shoulders jumped with surprise and she looked up from the book in her lap. "Hi!" she said, a smile spreading across her face. "You would really like this book, I think. It's about a girl and her cow, but there's also a dog in it." She showed me the cover. It looked pretty good.

"What's the cow's name?" I asked.

"Daisy," she answered, scooting over to make room for me on the rock.

I plopped down beside her. "I knew it! I feel like every cow in a book is named Daisy."

"Maybe it's, like, a rule or something," she said. "What would you name your cow?"

"Hmm." I thought about it. "Maybe Milkshake?"

"I'd name mine Moooooon," she said. We laughed.

I looked around the playground. "The buses are all here now. So where's Sadie?"

Isabel looked too. "Uh-oh. I hope she isn't sick today. She'd be sad to miss out on the cupcake party."

"Yeah," I said, "that would be too bad." Just

because I would be missing out on the fun didn't mean I wanted Sadie to miss it too.

"What would be too bad?" asked a familiar voice behind us. We turned and there was Sadie, looking not-at-all-sick after all. My worry floated away.

"We thought you might be absent and miss the party," Isabel explained.

"Nope!" Sadie said. "My dad dropped me off so I wouldn't have to carry Monica's present on the bus. I didn't want the ribbon to get crushed in my backpack."

I looked down and saw she was holding a medium-size box wrapped in shiny, colorful paper, with an enormous purple bow on top. Whatever the present was, it looked really fancy. Sadie placed it on the ground next to Isabel's and my backpacks, and shrugged off her own. I noticed she was wearing a special outfit—rainbow-striped leggings and a top covered with cupcakes.

Jealousy poked at my insides. They were going to have so much fun at the party without me.

"What did you get her?" Isabel asked.

"A Rainbow Loom," Sadie said. "She can use it to make bracelets and key chains and stuff."

The jealousy poked harder. I had always wanted one of those.

"I got her a book. It's the new Whatever After," Isabel said.

I looked down at my feet. I love that series. But it wasn't my birthday. Of course the presents weren't for me.

"Hey, guess what happened at breakfast this morning?" I said to change the subject. My friends both turned to listen. "Dad got so distracted thinking about the story he's writing, he poured orange juice into his coffee instead of milk!"

"Yuck!" Sadie said. "That sounds even worse than carrots in chocolate frosting."

"Yup. He took a sip before he noticed, and spit it right back out in the sink," I said. I smiled, remembering the surprised expression on Banana's face and the grossed-out one on Dad's. "Chuck said he'd pay me five bucks to drink it, but I said no way. I don't think he has five dollars, anyway." My brother always spends his allowance as soon as he's earned it. I was saving mine up to buy something special, but kept changing my mind about what the something special should be.

"Good call," Isabel told me.

Sadie squinted. "I wonder what kind of cupcakes we'll make at the party," she said. "I hope there's strawberry frosting." And just like that, they went back to talking about things that didn't include me.

I'd never been so glad to hear the first bell ring.

Chapter Three
Thumbs Up, Thumbs Down

When we got to our classroom, Sadie tucked the present into her cubbyhole and we settled at our desks as our teacher, Ms. Burland, clapped twice to start the day. I took out my pencils and lined them up at the top of my desk—first the regular yellow pencil I use for regular things, then the lucky blue pencil I use for spelling tests and quizzes, and finally the supersparkly rainbow pencil that's so special, I barely use it for anything at all. The supersparkly rainbow pencil always makes me happy when I look at it, and this morning was no exception. As I placed it on my desk, it glinted in the light and I instantly felt much better.

My mood improved even more when Ms. Burland handed back our math tests. Her shiny yellow shoes with black soles and black laces—the ones Banana and I call her bumblebee shoes— clicked on the floor as she walked between the rows of desks. When she reached mine, she said, "Nice job, Anna," and placed my test down. The grade at the top said 100. I glanced over at Isabel in the seat next to mine. She beamed back and gave me a thumbs-up.

Even the word of the day seemed determined to lift my spirits.

The word was "buoyant," which Ms. Burland pronounced like "boy-unt." It means "able to float" but also "cheerful and optimistic." I definitely felt more buoyant when I saw that.

I love the word of the day. It's one of the coolest things about being in Ms. Burland's class. We don't have to memorize it for a test or anything like that. Ms. Burland just writes it on the whiteboard for fun. I always tell Banana the day's word after school, and she perks up her ears for her favorites. I bet she would lift them extra high for this one.

I was still feeling good when the final bell rang to signal the end of the school day. But as I waited out front for Chuck to stop being a slowpoke so we could walk home together like usual, I watched Sadie and Isabel board the school bus with Monica and her other friends. They were smiling and laughing, holding presents and permission slips, and suddenly I didn't feel quite so buoyant.

Isabel turned at the bus door and gave me a quick wave. I waved back, but my mood had already sunk like a pebble tossed in a mud puddle.

Being left out was no fun at all.

Chapter Four
Never Have I Ever

Chuck finally came outside just as the bus with my friends on it drove away. "There you are! Yeesh. About time," he said, as if I were the one who'd been making him wait.

"Ha ha, very funny," I said. He grinned at his own joke and took off down the sidewalk. I followed. We were walking the opposite way from where the bus had gone, but at least each step brought me closer to Banana. "What took you so long, anyway?" I asked my brother.

"I was finishing a chess game. Claudia kicked my butt," he said. He was still grinning though.

Chuck was a surprisingly good loser. He never seemed to take things personally. I wondered where he'd gotten that talent. It was one I wished I had.

"Mr. Snyder lets you play games during school?" Sixth grade sounded awesome.

Chuck shook his head. "We had a sub, and I finished my science test early," he explained.

"Oh." We kept walking and I wondered what Sadie and Isabel were talking about on the bus ride to the party, and how long it would take them to get there. I wondered if they wished I were there with them or if they were having so much fun they'd forgotten me.

"Have you ever felt left out? Like everyone else was having fun without you?" I asked Chuck.

"Nope! Never," he said, and for a second I

almost believed him. "Bleep bleep bloop," he said, switching into a robot voice, and then I knew for sure he'd been teasing. "Does not compute." His body went stiff and he jerked back and forth as though his parts were made of metal. "Chuckle-bot 362SO does not feel hu-man e-mo-tions," he said, and I couldn't help but giggle.

Maybe Chuck was on to something. "Bleepity blop blop bloop," I said. I imagined my insides were filled with wheels and gears, like an old-fashioned clock. If I were made of metal, nothing could make me feel bad. That sounded pretty good right now. "What are hu-man e-mo-tions?" Robot-Anna asked.

"Bzzzzzzt! Brrrrrrrp! Bleeeeep!" Robot-Chuck whirred back. "Error! Error! File not found."

I pushed at the imaginary buttons on my stomach and followed my robot-brother home.

Chapter Five

Sweet and Sour

When we got to our house, Chuck and I powered out of robot mode and turned back into regular kids as we walked in the front door. Banana was right there waiting for me, like usual. She danced at our feet and barked hello, excited to see us. I crouched down to greet her with a kiss on the snout. Even a robot would be happy to see Banana. But I was glad to be human again so I could really feel her love.

Banana spun in a circle and made hopeful eyes at her leash, which was hanging on its hook by the door. I knew she wanted me to take her on a walk—or better yet, an adventure. Banana's favorite adventure these days was visiting our neighbor, Mrs. Shirley, and her new kitten, Surely Cat.

I liked visiting Mrs. Shirley and Surely Cat too. Banana and the kitten were slowly learning to get along, and it was fun watching them figure it out. Sometimes

Banana still got too eager and Surely Cat swiped her on the nose or hid where Banana couldn't reach him, but other times they both were happy to play chase or share a nap in an afternoon sunbeam. Mrs. Shirley was teaching me to play her favorite card games, and she almost always had cookies to share. Visiting my neighbor wasn't as special as decorating cupcakes at a birthday party, but it would still be fun.

I clipped on Banana's leash and called out, "We're going to Mrs. Shirley's!" and Banana and I set off down the block.

When we got to Mrs. Shirley's house, we stood on the doorstep and rang the buzzer again and again, but nobody answered. Mrs. Shirley wasn't home.

Banana's ears drooped with disappointment

as I led her away from the house. She'd really been looking forward to playing with her friend. "I know exactly how you feel," I told her. "I'm sorry." But there was nothing I could do to fix it.

Banana and I circled the rest of the way around the block until we found ourselves back home. I let us in the front door, feeling like my ears were drooping too.

"Back already?" Dad called from another room. "That was quick."

Banana and I followed the sound of his voice into the kitchen, where Dad was pouring more coffee into his TOP DOG mug.

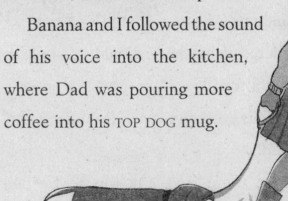

"Mrs. Shirley isn't home?" he guessed.

"Nope." I slid into a chair at the kitchen table and rested my chin in my hands. Banana laid down at my feet and heaved a big sigh. She sounded just as mopey as I  felt. I wondered if maybe I should go back to being a robot after all.

Dad lifted his eyebrows at us. "Bummer, huh?"

I shrugged.

"I suppose there isn't any fun to be had around here," he said. "No books to read, no games to play. Definitely no homework to do."

I twisted my mouth in response to his teasing. "At Mrs. Shirley's house there are cookies," I said.

"Oh." Dad took a sip from his mug. "Well, we don't have any cookies here."

I slumped down farther in my seat. Dad wasn't helping.

"We could make some though," he added.

I lifted my head. "We could?" I asked. Banana sat up and perked her ears.

"Sure," he said.

I jumped out of my chair and yelled, "Batter up!"

Chapter Six

Snickerdoo, Snickerdee

"All right," Dad said. "Step one in any baking project is to wash your hands thoroughly."

I ran to the sink and reached for the soap. Banana didn't have to wash her paws since she wouldn't be touching the food, but she ran to the sink alongside me, not wanting to miss out on the action. I dried my hands on a towel and Banana looked up at Dad as if to ask, *What's next?*

Dad tied back the strings on his favorite apron, the one that says STIRRING UP TROUBLE across the front. "Get your apron on too," he said. "And bring me that red cookbook off the shelf." I opened the drawer with the aprons inside, and Banana nosed at the one she thought I should wear— yellow with pink frosted donuts all over. I put it on, and chose a purple polka-dotted dishcloth to tie around Banana's neck, since we didn't have a doggy apron for her to wear. It looked more like a cape than an apron on her, but Banana lifted her snout proudly and Dad said, "Perfect. But now rewash your hands, please."

I almost protested—Banana wasn't dirty!— but she didn't look offended. I soaped up and rinsed off quickly, fetched the red cookbook, and carried it over to the counter. "Look up *snickerdoodles* in the index," Dad said. "It should be in alphabetical order."

I flipped to the

back of the book, snickering at the cookie's funny name, and found it listed under S. "Snickerdoodles, page 182," I said. Banana swished her tail.

"Great. Step two in baking is to make sure you have all the ingredients you'll need, before you start measuring or mixing any of them. Want to read them off to me?" Dad said.

"Butter, eggs, brown sugar, vanilla," I read out loud. "Flour, cinnamon, salt . . ." Banana tipped her head to one side, as if asking a question. I was wondering the same thing. *"Salt?"* I said. "That's weird. Do you think it's a mistake?"

Dad turned away from the cabinet, his arms full of ingredients. "Nope, not at all," he said. He set the things down on the counter. "Most desserts have a little salt in them—it brings out the flavor, even in sweet things. Just make sure you don't get the sugar and salt mixed up. That would *not* be delicious."

Banana stuck her tongue out. "Salty cookies, *blech*," I agreed.

"Ours won't be salty," Dad promised. "They'll be cinnamon-y and sweet. Now let's preheat the oven and butter these baking sheets, so the cookies won't stick to them. Then we can take turns measuring and stirring."

I got out the measuring cups and spoons, and Dad showed me how to run the flat edge of a knife across the top of a full measuring cup—to "level it off," he said, which means to scrape off the extra ingredients and make the measurement exact. Leveling off was Banana's favorite part of baking. Her eyes got wide as she watched the extra flour and sugar tumble from the measuring cup, back into their original containers. She was ready to catch any food that might fall toward the floor.

But despite Banana's hopes, we didn't drop any scraps. Dad cracked open the first egg and let me crack the second, and we mixed them with the butter, vanilla, and sugar, before adding the flour and spices. Soon I was rolling balls of cookie dough in a bowl of cinnamon sugar, to coat them with extra deliciousness, then lining them up on the baking sheets. I used two pot holders for safety and slid the first baking sheet into the oven.

Dad set a timer, and Banana and I turned on the oven light and watched through the little window as the cookies baked and baked. The longer

they were in there, the puffier they got, and the more delicious they smelled. I took a deep breath of the cinnamon-sugar air. I understood why Banana was drooling. I wished we could taste our cookies *right now*.

After what felt like a million minutes, the timer finally buzzed and I jumped up to grab the pot holders. With Banana waiting a safe distance away, Dad opened the oven door and I reached in to pull out the crackle-topped cookies. I put the baking sheet down on the cooling rack and gave Dad a big grin. It was almost time to eat them!

We lifted the second sheet of cookies out of the oven, then each chose one to try. I picked the one that looked most cinnamon-y.

I took my first bite of the warm, soft cookie. A burst of flavor filled my mouth. *"Mmm."*

"You're such a great helper. This might be the best batch of snickerdoodles I've ever made," Dad said.

I broke a piece off the one I'd been nibbling and gave a small taste to Banana. She licked her lips and agreed: The cookies had turned out perfectly.

I wasn't sad about missing out on the birthday party anymore—Banana and I had had too much fun baking with Dad for me to still be jealous about that. But I did wish I could share the yummy cookies I'd made with my friends.

I looked into the mixing bowl. There was still a little bit of cookie dough left. "Can we use the rest of the dough to make three extra-special, extra-big cookies for Sadie, Isabel, and me to have at lunch tomorrow?" I asked. "Please?"

Banana wagged her tail. She knew Sadie and Isabel would like that.

"Sure," Dad said. "That sounds like a sweet surprise."

Chapter Seven

The Way the Cookie Crumbles

The next morning I packed the three extra-special, extra-big snickerdoodles into my lunch bag, tucked the lunch bag into my backpack, and gave Banana three extra kisses on the nose before heading out the door to walk to school with Chuck.

Chuck had some snicker-doodles in his bag too. They were meant for him to eat later on with his hot lunch, but as soon as we were out of sight of the house, Chuck took them out of his backpack and stuffed them in his face.

"We're not supposed to eat cookies for breakfast," I told him.

"I'm not! I had Gorilla Grams for breakfast," he said with his mouth full. Crumbs flew in all directions as he talked. "This is my midmorning snack."

"It's not midmorning," I pointed out. "It isn't even eight o'clock yet."

Chuck shrugged. "So at midmorning I'll eat *your* cookies," he said and reached for my backpack.

"No way!" I slid my bag around to the front of my body to keep it away from Chuck's grabby hands. I knew he probably wouldn't really steal my cookies, but it was better to be safe than sorry.

He stuck out his lower lip and held up his hands like pretend paws in a begging position. "You won't share your cookies with a hungry wittle puppy?" he asked in his best sad-and-pitiful voice.

I laughed. It wasn't working. He'd been way more convincing as a robot. "Nope. They're good though, aren't they?"

He dropped his paws and his pout. "I don't remember. Let me taste one and I'll tell you!"

I rolled my eyes. I wasn't falling for that trick.

When we got to school, I found Sadie and Isabel out on the playground, swinging on the swings. I grabbed a swing next to them and kicked off against the ground. "How was the birthday party?" I asked.

"So much fun!" Sadie said.

"And tasty," Isabel added. "We each got to decorate six mini-cupcakes, and there were all these different flavor stations with choices for what kind of cake and frosting, plus a million different toppings to choose from."

"The toppings were amazing." Sadie pumped her legs to make her swing go higher. "There were mini-marshmallows and chocolate chips and crushed cookies and chopped-up candy bars, plus coconut and fruit and pretty much every color and shape of sprinkle you can think of."

"Don't forget the sauces," Isabel said.

"Oh yeah! There were bottles of caramel, butterscotch, and chocolate sauce too." Sadie licked her lips. "I made one with chocolate cake and chocolate frosting plus chocolate sprinkles, chocolate chips, *and* swirls of chocolate sauce on

top. Monica's mom called it
chocolate supreme."

"Wow," I said. "You guys
made all that?" The cookies
I'd made with Dad suddenly didn't seem all that
impressive.

Isabel twisted in her swing. "We didn't actually
bake anything. The cakes and frostings were all
premade. It was more like a decorating party than
a baking party, really. I guess we won't be going
on *The Batter-Up Bake-Off Show* anytime soon."

"Oh well," I said, but I was secretly relieved
they hadn't become master cupcake bakers without me. And now they'd be extra impressed by
my cookies. I couldn't wait to give them their
snickerdoodle surprise. I wished it were lunchtime already.

"I really like Monica," Sadie said. "She's so funny and sophisticated. We should invite her to hang out with us sometime."

"Yeah! She's awesome, right?" Isabel said. "She makes me laugh really hard."

My stomach did a little flip. Isabel laughed really hard when she was with us, too. We didn't need Monica for that.

I liked our threesome just the way it was. I didn't want to add someone I didn't know. But I knew it would sound grumpy and jealous to say so. "Sure," I said instead.

My friends didn't seem to notice that my smile was fake.

Chapter Eight

More Than a Mouthful

It was hard, but I kept the snickerdoodles a secret until lunchtime, so they could be a true surprise. When the bell rang, Sadie led the way to our favorite table in the cafeteria and plopped down in a seat next to the windows. Isabel and I put our lunches down and took the two seats across from her.

"I'm as hungry as a hippo," Sadie announced. We'd been playing Stop Hop at recess with Timothy and Justin, and by the end all our stomachs were growling. Sadie opened her lunchbox, took out each item, and arranged the food carefully in front of her. Even if she were eating her first meal in a week, Sadie would still be neat and organized about it.

"I'm as hungry as a dinosaur," Isabel said. She stabbed the straw into her juice box and a few red drops sprayed out onto the table. Sadie handed her a napkin.

"Dinosaurs don't get hungry! They're extinct," Sadie said.

Isabel shrugged and took a giant sip from her straw. "Fine, then I'm as hungry as a dragon," she said. She turned to me quickly, before Sadie could object again. "What about you, Anna?"

"I'm as hungry as Banana," I said. My friends laughed but I didn't mind. "You'd be surprised how much she can eat," I told them. Banana is just a little wiener dog, but she has a big appetite.

She always gets excited about food.

Sadie smiled around a mouthful of peanut butter and jelly. "Remember that kid at the party who dropped a cupcake in his soda and called it a cupcake float?" she asked. Isabel giggled and nodded, but I looked away. All day the conversation had kept coming back to *Monica's party this* and *Monica's party that*. The party was long over but I was still somehow getting left out of it. "Well, I'm so hungry, I would even eat *that*," Sadie said. She took another bite of her sandwich.

"You won't have to eat a soggy cupcake," I told her. "I brought you guys a special surprise for dessert."

Isabel clapped her hands together. "You did?"

"Yup." I pulled the three extra-big snickerdoodles out of my lunch bag. They were each in a separate baggie tied with a different color ribbon at the top. Banana had helped me choose the ribbons that morning. "They're called snicker-doodles," I said, handing Isabel the blue-ribbon one and Sadie the purple one. "I baked them yesterday."

"You made these? Wow," Isabel said.

Sadie looked impressed too. "When did you learn how to bake?" she asked.

My chest filled with pride, like a marsh-mallow puffing up in the microwave, but I shrugged like it was no big deal. "Dad taught me how. They're rolled in cinnamon-sugar," I said. "But the secret ingredient in cookies is salt."

"You're, like, an expert," Isabel said. "This looks delicious." She untied the ribbon and took her cookie out of its bag, not even finishing her sandwich first. She was just about to take a bite when Sadie started waving both arms at someone behind us.

Isabel put the cookie down and turned to look. Her face lit up with a smile. "Monica!" she shouted. "Over here!"

My stomach sank like an underbaked cake. Monica waved back to my two best friends and headed straight for our table.

Chapter Nine

Take a Bite

"Hey, you guys," Monica said as she came up behind me. She stuck her hand out over the middle of the table and she, Isabel, and Sadie did some kind of three-way high-five finger-wiggle move I

had never seen before. My stomach sank even further. Since when did they have a secret handshake? "Hi, Anna," she said, turning toward me like an afterthought.

"Hi," I replied. She didn't try the finger-wiggle move on me. I wasn't part of her *sophisticated* club.

"How's your baby panda?" she asked Isabel.

"Roly-poly roo!" Isabel sang out, and she, Sadie, and Monica burst into giggles. I had no idea what they were talking about, but nobody filled me in on the joke.

"Oooh, what's that?" Monica asked. She pointed at the snickerdoodle that was sitting on the table in front of me.

"Anna baked cookies!" Sadie held hers up for Monica to see. "They're called snickerdoodles. Want a piece of mine?"

"Sure," Monica said.

"No!" I shouted. I threw myself across the table, as fast and desperate as Banana leaping after a squirrel, to stop Sadie from breaking her cookie in half. Sadie froze and I realized all three of them were staring at me. My cheeks grew as hot as a preheated oven.

I straightened. "I mean . . . no, don't do that," I said, being careful not to shout this time. Sadie and Isabel still looked startled. Monica just looked confused.

The embarrassment spread from my cheeks to my ears. I knew I seemed really rude. But I'd made that cookie especially for Sadie. I didn't want her giving Monica half of it. "I, uh, I'm not hungry anymore. So here, you can have mine instead." I held out my own snickerdoodle for Monica to take.

"Really? Thanks! That's so nice of you," she said.

But I wasn't being nice. I was wishing she would disappear and leave my friends alone. She had plenty of her own friends—a whole birthday party's worth. Why did she need to take mine?

I watched, feeling miserable, as she untied the orange ribbon and took a bite of my cookie. "Wow, these are good," she said. "You really made them?" I nodded. My mouth watered, wishing for a taste of the cinnamon-y deliciousness, but there were no more cookies left for me.

Monica took another bite. "You should make these for the bake sale," she said.

"What bake sale?" Isabel asked.

"The one at the library this weekend. You all should come. It's on Saturday afternoon."

Sadie perked right up. "That's a great idea. We would totally win!"

Monica laughed. "The bake sale isn't a competition. It's to raise money for the library, so they can buy more books for the children's section."

"Oh. So then everybody wins," Isabel said. "I love the library."

Sadie nodded. "Me too. We'll definitely come, and we'll make cookies for it. Do you want to bake with us on Saturday morning?" she asked Monica.

Say no, say no, say no, say no, I thought. I

didn't want to be mean, but I also didn't want to bake cookies with her. I barely knew this girl, yet somehow she and my best friends had a secret handshake and inside jokes. I didn't want to include someone who made me feel so left out.

"I'd love to," Monica said, and my chest filled up with cement. "But I can't." The cement crumbled. "My troop is going early to help out with setup and stuff. But I'll see you there. I'm excited that you're coming!" She beamed at my friends and me and somehow I smiled back. "Thanks again for the cookie, Anna." She waved and walked away.

Isabel waved back. "Isn't she great?"

"Yeah. Great," I echoed.

I knew that friendship, like the bake sale, wasn't really a competition. But I couldn't help it: I wanted to win.

Chapter Ten
Chew on This

We each begged our parents for permission that night, and by morning the plan was set: On Saturday, Isabel's grandmother would drop her and Sadie off at my house before lunch. We would make snickerdoodles for the bake sale, with help from my dad, then he'd bring us to the library. When the bake sale was over, Sadie's mom would pick us up and we would have a sleepover at her house. It was going to be the best weekend ever. Banana and I couldn't wait.

But when I got to school on Friday morning, I discovered what my Nana would call a hitch in the plans.

"Monica says her troop is making strawberry lemonade for the bake sale tomorrow," Isabel reported when I joined her and Sadie on the playground.

"Yum. I love strawberry lemonade," Sadie said. "I wonder if they'll serve it with little umbrellas, like in the drinks at Monica's party. Wasn't that fancy?"

I didn't say anything. I hadn't seen the fancy umbrellas, since I wasn't invited to the party. And I was tired of hearing about Monica.

"And she and her mom baked chocolate chip cookies to sell," Isabel said. She dropped down from the mon-key bars, landing on the ground beside me. "She

said they put cinnamon in the batter to make it extra delicious."

I stared at her. "Monica put cinnamon in her cookies?"

"Yup," Isabel confirmed. I could tell she didn't see what the problem was, but I couldn't believe Monica had done that.

"But . . . *our* cookies will have cinnamon in them. She knows that!" I said.

"So?" Isabel said, but Sadie was frowning. She understood why I was upset.

"We want our cookies to be special," Sadie said. "What was that word of the day? The one that means one-of-a-kind?"

"Unique," I said.

"Yeah. We want our cookies to be unique and also the most delicious. Then we'll sell the most," Sadie said.

Isabel tilted her head, like Banana does when she has a question. "But Monica said the bake sale isn't a competition. It's about helping the library, not being the best."

"Yeah, but the better our cookies are, the more money the library gets. So really, it's about both," Sadie said. She tucked a few stray curls into her ponytail, and climbed up the jungle gym ladder.

Isabel rolled her eyes and gave me a little smile that said *Sadie always gets so competitive.* I smiled back, but I secretly wanted us to bake the best thing too—or at least, I wanted our cookies to sell better than Monica's. I was glad to hear Sadie was thinking of us as a team though—a team without Monica on it. "Sadie's right. We want our cookies to be special," I said. "If Monica's have cinnamon, we should make something else."

"How about peanut butter cookies? I love those," Sadie said.

"Or oatmeal raisin?" Isabel said.

I shook my head. For all we knew, someone else could be baking those kinds too.

Sadie hooked her legs over the monkey bars and released her hands so she was hanging upside down. "I know!" she said. "Let's make up our own recipe! That's how they do it on *The Batter-Up Bake-Off Show*."

"Yeah, but those kids are expert bakers," Isabel said.

"Anna's an expert," Sadie said, just as the first bell rang. She pulled herself right-side up and started climbing down. "Do you think you could do it, Anna?"

I hesitated. I definitely knew I could bake delicious snickerdoodles, especially with Dad's help, and I could probably follow another recipe just as well. But that didn't mean I could make up something even better. I was about to say so, when I heard a voice behind us.

"Sadie! Guess what?" Monica called from where she was lining up to go inside with the rest of Mr. Garrison's class. "My parents said I can go to the sleepover!"

"Yay!" Sadie shouted back. She picked up her backpack off the ground.

"You invited Monica to the sleepover? That's great!" Isabel said.

Sadie nodded and looked at me. "So, what do you think?" she asked.

I took a deep breath and pulled my shoulders straight. "I think we're going to invent the best cookie recipe ever."

Chapter Eleven

The Taste of Regret

Isabel jumped up and down and let out a whoop. Sadie high-fived us both and said, "This will be awesome!" I followed my friends into our classroom and felt my smile stretch from ear to ear.

But when I took my seat and looked up at the word of the day, my smile shrank. The word was "exaggerate." *Exaggerate: to make something seem bigger, better, or worse than it truly is.* A funny feeling itched at the center of my chest, like it was being tickled by the tip of Banana's tail. I couldn't scratch away this feeling though. It came from the inside.

My promise to invent a new cookie recipe had made my friends happy, so I was glad I'd said it—but I was worried I wouldn't be able to do it. I knew I had exaggerated my baking skills. I wasn't really an expert baker. I was only a beginner. How was I supposed to come up with a recipe so delicious and unique it would win the whole bake sale?

I knew I should tell Isabel and Sadie *never mind*, that I had made a mistake and we should stick with the snickerdoodles after all. They would be disappointed, for sure. But they were my friends. They would understand. It wouldn't make them decide they liked Monica better. At least, I hoped it wouldn't.

But I didn't tell them right then, while Ms. Burland handed back spelling tests, because

Sadie was whispering to Amanda, who sits in front of her, and whatever she said made Amanda turn and give me a big thumbs-up.

I didn't tell them during science because we were reading aloud about liquids, solids, and gases. After my turn to read, Isabel tilted her notebook to show me what she'd been drawing—a picture of Banana wearing a little chef's hat, in front of a shop called Anna's Bakery. The sign in the window said WORLD'S BEST BANANA BREAD!

Justin leaned over my shoulder and said, "Anna's Bakery? What's that?" Before I could stop her, Isabel told him I

was a world-class baker and would be inventing an amazing new cookie for the bake sale. "Cool," Justin said. And then he told Keisha.

I put my head down on my desk. This was getting out of control.

By the time the bell rang for recess, everyone knew about the cookies. Our whole entire class expected my new recipe to be the very best thing at the bake sale. Ms. Burland even said she would be there to try it.

I couldn't back out now. I had to invent a new cookie, and just hope it wouldn't be a disaster.

Chapter Twelve

In My Expert Opinion

When I got home from school, I clipped on Banana's leash and told her all my worries as we walked around the block. Banana looked up at me with big eyes and wagged her tail in sympathy. She didn't know how to fix my problem, but it still felt good to tell her about it. Banana's a really good listener.

We circled back to the house and found Chuck in the kitchen, eating the last of the snickerdoodles. "Don't worry, I saved you one," he said. "But only because Dad said I had to."

"Gee, thanks." I poured myself a glass of milk

and set it down next to my cookie. Chuck picked it up, took a swig, and gargled the milk before swallowing. "You're disgusting," I informed him.

Chuck flashed a smile that showed all his teeth. "Thank you," he said.

"Hey, if you were inventing a new kind of cookie, what would you put in it?" I asked.

"Hmmm." Chuck scrunched up his face while he thought about it. "Oh! I know— grasshoppers," he said.

"Ew." I already regretted asking him.

"Yeah, I guess grasshoppers are too crunchy. So maybe worms?" he said.

"Chuck, I'm being serious," I said.

"Okay, fine. I would use . . . honey," he said.

Banana lifted her ears. I agreed, honey cookies sounded tasty. "And mashed bees," he added.

I gave him a shove. "Thanks a lot."

He burped. Banana tucked her tail between her legs. Even she'd had enough of Chuck's grossness.

Dad walked into the kitchen, loosening the tie he always wears for work. Dad is a writer so he works at home where nobody but us sees him. If he wanted, he could wear a space suit and flip-flops, or a hat made of tin foil, but Dad says the tie helps him focus. He pulled it off now and draped it over the back of a chair, and I knew he was done with his writing for the day.

"Who wants to help grate cheese for the tacos?" Dad asked.

Chuck and Banana both sat straight up.

Chuck loves tacos almost as much as Banana loves cheese. "I do!" he said.

Banana barked in agreement, and Dad laughed. He reached down to pet her. "I'm sure you'd be very helpful, Banana, but we'll let Chuck take cheese duty tonight," he said. "Anna, will you set the table for dinner, please?"

"Okey-doke." I slid off the chair and went to open the silverware drawer. Dad put on some music and tied his apron strings. By the time Mom walked in and took off her work shoes, the whole house smelled delicious.

I piled my first taco high with extra tomatoes and cheese, letting a few scraps fall to the floor for Banana as I took a giant bite. We're not supposed to feed Banana people food at the table, but it was mostly an accident, sort of. Besides,

Mom and Dad break that rule sometimes too. It's very, very hard to say no to Banana's begging because she's very, very cute, which makes her very, very good at it.

Mom and Dad weren't really paying attention to what I was doing though. They were too busy talking about Mom's busy work day and the client she was helping to "build their brand" and "maximize customer loyalty."

Under the table, Banana leaned against my leg and nudged me hard with her snout. At first I thought she wanted more cheese, but then she nudged me again and I realized what she was saying. She was right: The person I should be asking about my cookie question wasn't Chuck, it was Mom. Mom's the boss at her office and a super-smart business person. She'd for sure know how to help me sell the most cookies.

I thanked Banana for her good idea with another scrap of cheese, and waited until Mom and Dad had finished talking, so I wouldn't get scolded for interrupting.

"Hey, Mom," I said as soon as I had the chance. "If a client asked your advice on how to really stand out, like how to make sure the thing they're selling is better than what anybody else is selling, what would you tell them?"

Mom raised both eyebrows like she was surprised at the question, but she didn't ask why I was wondering. "Well," she said, and I could tell from her face that she was thinking seriously about her answer, "I'd probably tell them, 'You should play to your strengths.' My advice would be to figure out what sets you and your product apart and makes it special, then focus on that and run with it." She took a sip of water. "Does that make sense?"

"I think so," I said, even though I wasn't sure yet. But then I got it: What made our cookies special was that Sadie, Isabel, and I would be baking them together, and we're a really good team. So our brand new, one-of-a-kind recipe should show off how great the three of us were together.

Thinking about it that way, I knew exactly what kind of cookie we should invent.

"Does this have anything to do with tomorrow's bake sale?" Dad asked.

I reached down to scratch Banana behind her ears, and nodded at Dad's question. "Yup. I think we're going to need a few more ingredients."

Chapter Thirteen
An Unwanted Ingredient

On Saturday morning, I woke up to sunshine peeking through the window blinds and Banana snoring softly in her basket beside my bed. I slid out from under the covers quietly, trying not to

wake her, but the second my feet touched the floor, Banana opened her eyes and thumped her tail against the cushion in her basket. She was excited for bake sale day too.

After my breakfast of Gorilla Grams with milk and Banana's breakfast of kibble, we hurried through my chores. By the time I'd finished straightening my room and vacuuming the whole upstairs, Dad had returned from the grocery store and it was almost time for my friends to arrive.

Banana perked up her ears at the sound of Isabel's family minivan pulling into our driveway. We ran outside. I waved to Abuelita in the driver's seat and she waved back as Sadie and Isabel climbed out of the car.

Banana jumped at their feet, yipping hello. I

was bouncing up and down too, I was so happy to see them. I couldn't wait for us to try out my cookie invention. We were going to have a great day, even though it would end with Monica being at the sleepover too. But by then Sadie, Isabel, and I would have already rocked the bake sale together, as a team. It would be clear to everyone, including Monica, that we were complete as a threesome.

Banana barked again and Isabel turned back to the minivan. I thought she would shut the door, but instead she said something I couldn't hear to a third person who was stepping out of the car and onto my driveway. I stared. It was Monica.

She grinned. "Hi, Anna! We finished the setup early, so it turns out I can bake with you guys after all." A funny look crossed her face and she added, "I hope that's okay."

I realized I was still staring at her with my mouth hanging open. I forced my jaw to shut and tried to push my lips up at the corners. It didn't quite work.

"Of course," I said. But it wasn't okay.

It wasn't okay with me at all.

Chapter Fourteen
Salt in the Wound

Isabel led the way up the steps and into my house, with Sadie and Monica following and Banana right at their heels. I stood outside alone for a second, watching them all disappear inside as if they didn't even notice I wasn't with them. Banana poked her nose back out and I heard Sadie call, "Come on, Anna!" and slowly my heart started beating again. I took a deep breath and walked inside.

Monica looked right at home in my house already. She plopped down on the carpet, sitting crisscross-apple-sauce with my two best friends on either side of her. Banana bounded over to them and Monica scratched her under the chin, in the special spot where Banana likes to be petted. Banana wagged her whole backside with delight.

Even Banana thought Monica was great. It felt like such a betrayal.

Dad came into the living room, wiping his hands on a dishcloth. "Hello, hello," he said to Sadie and Isabel. His gaze landed on Monica. "Oh! And hello to you too," he added.

"Dad, this is Monica. Monica, this is my dad," I said. "She's how we knew about the bake sale in the first place," I explained.

Dad gave her a big smile and said, "Welcome." I

wished there were some kind of signal I could flash, one to say he shouldn't be *too* friendly, that Monica wasn't supposed to be here and I didn't want her baking cookies with us. But I wasn't sure how to do that without being the rudest person ever. Besides, Dad would probably just signal back that I should stop being a spoilsport and start being a good host. I decided to try.

"Are you hungry?" I asked Monica. "Dad's making us turkey sandwiches with veggie sticks and dip."

"Yum!" Monica said. She turned to Isabel. "Remember that time at lunch last year when we made a log cabin out of carrots and celery?"

Isabel nodded and Banana wagged and Sadie said, "That sounds awesome."

I sighed and went into the kitchen alone.

Chapter Fifteen
A Little of This, a Little of That

I stayed pretty quiet during lunch, but if either of my friends noticed I wasn't talking, they didn't comment on it. Monica, Isabel, and Sadie had plenty to say to each other, so it wasn't like the room was silent. Banana noticed, though. She stayed close by my feet and at one point even leaned against my leg to help me feel less lonely. When I finished my sandwich, I let her lick the mayonnaise and crumbs off my fingers, then stroked her soft ears. It helped.

Dad walked into the kitchen and chomped on a celery stick. "Who's ready to do some baking?" he asked.

"I am!" Isabel said, jumping up to clear our empty dishes. Monica stood up to help, and a small piece of carrot rolled off her plate. Banana lunged to catch it. She crunched it between her teeth and looked up at Monica like she was her new best friend. I turned away.

Dad was already putting on his apron. I realized I hadn't exactly told him we wanted to bake the cookies without his help. With Monica here, that seemed extra important. "Please please please can we do this on our own?" I asked. "It's for the library! And our recipe is top secret."

Dad hesitated, and I tried to make my eyes as big and round as Banana's get when she begs. "Okay, but you know the rules: no sharp knives and no playing with fire," he said.

"We promise," I said.

He folded up his apron and stuck it back in the drawer. "Holler if you need me. I'll be right over there in the other room."

"We will," I said.

I heard Monica whisper to Isabel, "Playing with fire?"

"He means don't use the oven without him," I explained.

"Oh," she said. "We have that rule at my house too."

I stood up straight and took charge. "Step one in baking is to thoroughly wash your hands," I announced. "And everyone gets an apron, even Banana." I tied the purple polka-dotted dishcloth around Banana's neck, and chose the three nicest aprons for Sadie, Isabel, and me. I dug to the bottom of the drawer to find the plain beige

apron no one in my family ever wears because it isn't fun colors, plus it has a few ugly stains on the front. I handed that one to Monica.

"Thanks," she said and put it on without complaint. I nodded and took my turn at the sink.

"Step two is to get out all the ingredients we'll need—so now you get to see what's in our top secret, brand new recipe!" I said as I dried my clean hands on a towel.

I dragged a stepping stool over to the cabinet and started taking out the ingredients we'd need and handing them to Isabel and Sadie to place on the counter. Banana licked her lips.

"These cookies are called Sanabels," I said. "As in SA-die, An-NA, Isa-BEL." I gave

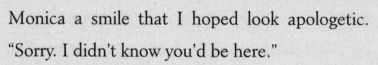

Monica a smile that I hoped look apologetic. "Sorry. I didn't know you'd be here."

"That's okay." Monica said it so nicely I almost felt bad. But it wasn't my fault she'd crashed our baking party.

"There are three special ingredients in Sanabels, one for each of us," I said. "Peanut butter for Sadie, oatmeal for Isabel, and bananas for me—well, and for Banana," I added. Banana wagged her approval.

"Mmm, peanut-butter-oatmeal-banana cookies sound great!" Sadie said.

Monica nodded. "I bet those flavors will go really well together."

Exactly. Just like how Sadie, Isabel, and I went well together. Monica totally got it. It almost made me like her.

"Should we add chocolate chips, too?" Isabel asked. "Chocolate would taste good in there, I bet. And then there'd be four special flavors, for the four of us."

"No! I already invented the cookie." I jumped down from the stepping stool. "Besides, we don't have any chocolate chips," I added, even though that probably wasn't true. But I didn't want to add a fourth special ingredient to the cookies—the fourth person wasn't even supposed to be here.

Banana flattened her ears and Sadie frowned, while Isabel shifted from foot to foot. I opened the refrigerator so I wouldn't have to look at any of their faces. If they were feeling sorry for

Monica, I didn't want to know it. She'd left me out of her private jokes, her secret handshake, and her cupcake party. Why should I have to include her in my recipe?

"Want help?" Monica asked as I loaded up my arms with ingredients.

"Nope. I've got it." I turned and tried to shut the refrigerator door with my toe.

"Here, let me take the eggs." Monica put her hand on the carton.

I jerked away. "I said I've got it!"

But right as I said that, the egg carton fell from my arms and crashed to the floor with a *splat*.

Chapter Sixteen

Turning Up the Heat

"Oh no!" Sadie cried. She ran to pick up the carton but it was already a soggy mess. Banana ran to lap up the egg whites that had leaked out onto the floor. I didn't run anywhere—I was too stunned to move. What if all the eggs were cracked?

"I'm sorry. I'm so sorry. I didn't mean to do that," Monica said. She looked just as upset as I felt.

My heart thudded fast and I wanted to scream, *Well, if you hadn't tried to help me, I wouldn't have dropped them!* But the words echoed in my head before they came out, and I could hear how silly they sounded. I clamped my lips shut. My face felt hot with shame.

I stared at my feet. "It wasn't your fault. I'm the one who moved too quickly," I mumbled. Though it was a little bit her fault too, I thought. If Monica hadn't been here, none of this would have happened.

Dad appeared in the doorway. "Everything all right in here? I thought I heard an *oh no*."

"We dropped the eggs," Isabel explained. She and Sadie opened the carton over the sink. Sadie wrinkled her nose and Isabel cringed. "They're all broken," she said.

"Uh-oh," Dad said. He looked at the clock. "We don't have time to get to the store and back. The bake sale starts in an hour."

My insides tumbled with panic. Without eggs,

we couldn't make any cookies. The whole recipe would be ruined. What were we going to do?

Monica peeked over Sadie's shoulder into the egg carton. "Maybe we can save some of what's left. Do you have a bowl?" she asked.

I got out a cereal bowl and brought it over to where they were standing. Monica reached into the carton and pulled out half an egg shell. She tipped its contents into the bowl. "That's half an egg," she said. "How many do we need?"

"Two," I said. Banana sat at my feet, right below the egg bowl, and looked up, her eyes as round as yolks.

Isabel picked up another broken egg and put

that in the bowl too. "Half plus half equals one. We'll have to fish out that piece of shell, though."

Hope blasted through my body like a sugar rush. "This might work!" I gave Monica a grateful smile. She smiled back. Maybe we hadn't ruined everything.

Dad nodded. "I think it will. Ready to preheat that oven, then?"

Dad helped me with the oven while Isabel, Monica, and Sadie rescued what we hoped added up to be two whole eggs, and fished out the broken eggshell with a spoon. I got out the mixing bowls and measuring cups, and showed the others how to scoop up and level off the flour and oats, while Banana showed them how to watch for any falling ingredients. Sadie stirred in the peanut butter while I cut up two bananas and Isabel sang a silly song she'd made up on the spot. Monica splashed in the milk, Isabel added the pinch of salt, and we all joined in the chorus: "Da-da-dee, da-da-dum, cookie time, yum-yum-yum!" We took turns stirring the batter with a big wooden spoon. Baking with friends was even more fun than I'd thought it would be.

"Can we taste the dough?" Isabel asked.

"No, we shouldn't, not until it's baked.

Eating raw eggs can be dangerous," Sadie said.

I hadn't known that about eggs, but I nodded like I did, since I was supposed to be the baking expert.

"It looks sooooo good," Monica said. "I can't believe you made this up, Anna! Everyone's going to be super impressed." I was glad she thought so. I thought it too.

We greased the cookie sheets, scooped out spoonfuls of dough, and rolled them into little balls. When the dough balls were all lined up on the cookie sheets, I showed everyone how to flatten them with our palms.

Isabel giggled. "Squishing the cookies is my favorite part!"

Sadie grinned. "My favorite part is going to be *eating* them."

I called Dad in to help us put the cookies in the oven, then we set the timer and put away all the ingredients while we waited for the cookies to bake. Soon the kitchen smelled like peanut-butter-oatmeal-banana deliciousness. My mouth watered and Banana was already starting to beg. I couldn't wait to try them.

When the timer went off, Dad pulled the cookie sheets out of the oven using two thick pot holders, and set them on a rack to cool. When we couldn't wait another second longer, I used a metal spatula to lift up one of the cookies and split it into four pieces. "The first Sanabel!" I said, and handed out the quarters.

I watched as Isabel put her whole piece in her mouth and chewed. Her eyebrows scrunched together and her smile dropped. Beside her,

Sadie spit a chewed-up mouthful back out into her palm. Monica swallowed her bite politely then ran to get a drink of water.

Banana's eyes seemed to say exactly what I was thinking: *Oh no, oh no, oh no.*

Chapter Seventeen

Taste Test Time

I lifted the warm piece of cookie to my lips and forced myself to try it. I closed my eyes as I mashed the too-hard Sanabel between my teeth. It was tough and dry and not at all like what I'd imagined when I invented the recipe. It didn't even taste like a cookie, really. Cookies were supposed to taste *good*.

I swallowed down the disappointing bite and opened my eyes. Everyone was staring at me, even Banana. My cheeks turned hot with embarrassment. "That's not what they're supposed to taste like," I said. "I don't know what went wrong."

"Aren't cookies usually . . . sweeter?" Monica asked.

I groaned. "Oh no. That's it! I forgot the sugar." I sank down to the floor and sat with my face in my hands. So much for my being an expert baker.

Banana tried to lick my ear but I moved away from her tongue. I didn't want her to comfort me. I didn't deserve her pity. "How could I have done that? This is a total disaster." But deep down, I knew how it had happened. I'd been so worked up about Monica, I couldn't focus on anything else. I wished I could blame her for that, but I could only blame myself.

"It's okay, Anna. We'll just make another batch," Isabel said.

I dropped my hands to my lap and looked up at her. "We can't! We'd never get them done in time. Besides, we're out of eggs and the cookies won't work without those, either."

"Maybe some people will like them anyway. Not everyone wants to eat sweet things," Sadie said. But she didn't sound like she believed it.

I shook my head. "They taste like dog food—maybe worse. We can't sell these. I'm sorry. I ruined everything."

Monica laughed. For a second I thought she must be the meanest person in the world, laughing at my failure like that. But then she said, "Like dog food! That's perfect!" and gave me an excited smile. "We can sell them as dog treats! People—and pups—will love it."

Sadie jumped up and down. "Yes! Great idea!"

Isabel broke a piece off one of the cookies and tossed it in the air. "What do you think, Banana?"

Banana leaped to catch the treat in her mouth. She swallowed it, spun in a happy circle, and stood up on her hind legs, begging for more.

"She loves it!" Sadie said.

"Hooray for Sanabel dog biscuits! They'll be gobbled up in no time," Monica said.

I stood up. "Actually, I think we should call them Sanabelicas," I said. "For SA-die, An-NA, Isa-BEL, and Mon-ICA."

Monica looked at me shyly. "Are you sure?" she asked.

"Positive. After all, you saved the day—twice! We couldn't have done it without you," I said.

"Yeah!" Isabel cheered at the same time Sadie said, "True!" Isabel held up her hand for a four-way high-five, and Monica showed me the finger-wiggle move I had seen them all do at lunchtime. After two tries, I got it. It was pretty cool.

"I'm glad you're here," I told her, and I meant it.

Chapter Eighteen

Dog Tested, Brother Approved

When the Sanabelicas had cooled, we packed them in a cookie tin to bring to the bake sale. Chuck walked into the kitchen, holding a stack of library books to return. "Dad says to tell you it's almost time to go," he said. "Ooooh, cookies! Don't mind if I do." He helped himself to a dog treat before I could stop him.

Sadie's mouth hung wide open and Banana's tail shot straight up, but Monica caught my eye as Chuck chewed and swallowed, and we burst into giggles. "What?" Chuck said. We laughed even harder.

Chuck rolled his eyes. "Weirdos." He snatched another dog treat and left the room.

"We should make a sign: Sanabelicas! The perfect treat for your dog . . . or your brother," Sadie said.

Sanabelicas!
The perfect treat
for your dog...
or your brother

"Yes!" Isabel grabbed a marker out of the pen jar on the counter.

"That's totally something my older brother would do too," Monica said. "If I bring some home for Nickels, I'll probably have to hide them from Diego."

Isabel looked up from the sign she was making. "Nickels is her dog. Diego is the brother," she explained.

"You have a dog? And a brother?" I asked. Monica nodded. "Cool!" I hadn't realized we had so much in common.

"Nickels and Banana should get together sometime. It would be really cute to watch them play," Monica said.

Banana wiggled her whole backside at the idea of a new friend. "Totally," I agreed.

Banana and I ran upstairs to get my overnight bag for the sleepover, while Isabel finished the sign and Monica and Sadie finished the kitchen cleanup. When we came back downstairs, Dad was jiggling his car keys. He looked inside the cookie tin and read Isabel's sign. "Dog biscuits, huh? Great idea," he said. "What's the secret ingredient?"

"Friendship," I said.

Monica winked. "And teamwork," she added.

Dad tossed his keys in the air then caught them. "Sounds like a perfect combination," he said.

I smiled at my three friends and Banana. "It is."

Acknowledgments

Like baking, writing a story is even more fun when it is done with or for friends, and the Anna, Banana books are for sure a team effort. I am grateful to everyone at S&S who helps stir the pot, including editor Alexa Pastor (who knows just the right spices to include), editrix emeritus Kristin Ostby, art director Laurent Linn, publicist Audrey Gibbons, production editor Katrina Groover, production manager Martha Hanson, publisher Justin Chanda, and deputy publisher Anne Zafian. Meg Park's illustrations are a key not-so-secret ingredient. My agent, Meredith Kaffel Simonoff, knows when to add sugar and when to add salt. (She is one smart cookie.)

Thank you to my family—especially Mama, Ati, Jeff, Jeremy, Erika, Anna, and Sophia—for encouraging even my most unusual concoctions. And thank you to my friends, who provide the best kinds of nourishment, and Arugula Badidea, who stirs up the cutest trouble.

The best thing about writing a story is knowing a reader might gobble it up. Thank *you*, reader, for choosing this book. I hope you found it tasty.

Turn the page for a sneak peek
at the next book in the series,
ANNA, BANANA, AND THE
SLEEPOVER SECRET

Pajama Plans

"Which pajamas should I bring: the rainbow pair or the pony pair?" I asked, peering into the top drawer of my dresser.

My dog, Banana, tipped her head to one side as she considered the question.

"The rainbow ones are softer, but the pony ones are newer," I said. I grabbed both pairs and held them out for inspection. Banana sniffed each one, then nudged my left hand with her snout.

I grinned. "Rainbows it is." I returned the ponies to their drawer and tucked the rainbow pajamas into my backpack, on top of the toothbrush, hairbrush, underwear, socks, shirt, leggings, glow-in-the-dark clawed dragon-feet slippers, and sparkly nail polish that I had already packed for the sleepover. I went to my closet and stood on tiptoe to pull my sleeping bag off its high shelf, and as I turned back around with it, I heard a familiar squeak. I looked down and saw Banana holding her favorite toy, a yellow plastic bunny, in her mouth. She wagged her tail hopefully, and bit down to make it squeak again.

I bent to take it from her, and tossed it across the room. It landed in the doggy basket right next to my bed, where Banana always sleeps. She bounded over to retrieve it, and carried it back to me proudly. She dropped it at my feet and looked up at me, hoping I would throw it for her again.

I knew this game: Banana wanted to distract me from packing. I hesitated, and she nosed at the toy, pushing it toward me.

I gave in. "I can't play all day," I warned her as I flicked the bunny high into the air. "Isabel's expecting us to come over soon."

Banana jumped to catch the toy before it could fall to the ground, and carried it over to my open backpack. She dropped the bunny inside. I laughed, but I also felt a twinge of guilt as I took the toy back out. "I'm sorry," I told her. "By 'us' I meant Sadie and me. I can't bring you to the sleepover. Unfortunately, dogs aren't invited."

Isabel's giant orange tabby cat, Mewsic, doesn't get along well with other animals, so it wouldn't be fair to bring Banana into Mewsic's home. We had discussed this already and I knew Banana understood that I would include her in the sleepover if I could, but that didn't stop her ears from drooping with disappointment.

I squeezed the yellow bunny, hoping its squeaks would cheer her up, and tossed it as hard as I could. Banana watched as the bunny sailed over her head and landed on the other side of the room, but she didn't even try to chase it.

"Aw, I'm going to miss you too," I said. I dropped to my knees and nuzzled my face against her soft fur. "But it's only for one night. I'll be back tomorrow morning with lots of stories to tell."

Banana's ears perked back up. She loves a good story.

"Knock knock," a voice said. Banana and I looked up to see my mom standing in the open doorway to my room. She was wearing the oversize sweatshirt my brother, Chuck, and I had given her for her last birthday. It was supersoft and had big pockets where she could put her hands if they got cold. Mom's fingers were always freezing. "You all packed for the sleepover?" she asked. I nodded. "Good. You've got just enough time for a quick lunch before Sadie's dad picks you up. Come on downstairs. Dad's making grilled cheese."

"Cheese!" I cheered, and Banana twirled in a circle, chasing her own tail with excitement. She loves cheese almost as much as she loves stories.

Banana led the way out of my room and I raced down the stairs after her. We both knew

I would sneak her a small bite of cheese if I got the chance. I wasn't really supposed to feed her at the table, of course, but Mom and Dad didn't have to know.

It would be our little secret.

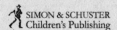

JOIN THIRD-GRADE SCIENTIST AND
INVENTOR EXTRAORDINAIRE ADA LACE AS SHE
SOLVES MYSTERIES USING SCIENCE AND TECHNOLOGY!

"Come catch me! I dare you!"

When a golden leaf teases Patches, dancing just out of reach, the little house cat can't resist. So away she goes—chasing the leaf out into the great, wide world, on a journey her heart tells her she must follow.

But the great outdoors is bigger than Patches ever could have imagined.

Want to know what dogs are thinking?
What they feel, and what they can smell
with that great big nose of theirs?
This book, by dog owner and scientist
Alexandra Horowitz, is as close as you can get to
knowing about dogs without *being* a dog yourself.

INSIDE *of a* DOG
WHAT DOGS SEE, SMELL, AND KNOW
ALEXANDRA HOROWITZ

Young Readers Edition

PRINT AND EBOOK EDITIONS AVAILABLE
From Simon & Schuster Books for Young Readers
simonandschuster.com/kids